WEATHERED HEART

by

Nesta Rüegg-Aberdeen

26/8/16   **Silent Pain**

To darling Wilped, ☺
Thankyou for your lovely
Company + everything you
are. Much love + appreciation
Nesta ♡

ISBN: 1-905451-33-4

A CIP catalogue for this book is available from the National Library.

This book was published in cooperation with
Choice Publishing & Book Services Ltd, Ireland
Tel: 041 9841551 Email: info@choicepublishing.ie
www.choicepublishing.ie

Sometimes I feel I could break down
and cry
Sometimes I try so hard to hide the
pain
The tears I cannot find

DEDICATION

HEART

You let me suffer the pains of love
But showed me the joys of loving
Let me rejoice in the morning
Give praise in the evening
For this warm and wonderful feeling
Let me forget not the passion
The sweetness, dear heart
You let me know love
As no other heart has ever known
You let me take another heart
And make it my own
Without you, I'm lost on my own
Heart, let me not alone

To my two beautiful hearts, Stefan and Sabrina, unaware
as they are, for exposing me to the real pain, allowing me
to see that pain is so much more than it seems and that the
greater part of pain is joy

Introduction

Weathered Heart is a collection for lovers, especially those who have loved and learned from the pain.

In this, her first anthology , Nesta wanders back and forth across her very intense emotional frontiers, recalling childhood longings, conjuring up dreams and fantasies, and reliving the realization of womanhood.

The pieces in this anthology are a testimony to the frailty of the human condition, expressed by such themes like the fear of being forsaken, the hurt that loneliness brings, the deep unfulfilled longing to laugh and sing,

> "To reach deep within
> Touch my happiness
> And know that it´s real"

and the liberating power of tears that women know.

In spite of the tears however, the anthology at times project the spirit of joy, a quiet joy in the beauty of things and the comforting peace that comes with accepting things as they are, as in **Best Friends**:

> "If we can´t be together
> Let´s not lose each other
> Let´s be friends
> After all
> Best friends are the second best"

or the victory of the human spirit even in death in **If I should die**

"The clouds cry
The sun shines
The flowers grow
And the earth flourishes
Into a paradise"

All in all, weathered heart is a very deep journey inward and the collection might well have been called Narratives of the heart. I congratulate Nesta for this very fine first anthology.

Chris DeRiggs
Playwright and Director of Heritage Theatre Company

WEATHERED HEART

THE WRITINGS

DREAM A DREAM OF LOVE FOR 2

Sitting out one cold dark night
Nothing to comfort me
A drink in my hand, a song in my heart
But no one to hear my song
No one to hold me tight

The stars above are few
Looking down on me and listening too, to the rhythm of
my heart
The silence is plenty and so too is my loneliness
caressing me

High is the moon
A long, drawn face
Standing alone in its place
And its soft glow promises the hope of a new dawn
Alas! A star, shooting afar
In a twinkle I see a star shooting down on me
My long-face friend no doubt has seen it too
And on that star a wish was made
Somehow wishes really do come through
Like miracles really do happen
'Cause in my heart awakening
A magical, warm embrace
A new song
And that night
While in my bed I lie
I close my eyes and dream…
A dream of love for two

YOU ARE MY STAR

A single candle on the Christmas tree
Lights up the whole room
You light up my life
Like the day and the night
You are the sun
I am the moon
A smile from you is like sunshine in my heart
You warm my days
And my whole world seems bright
Of all the stars at night
That fill the sky and shine so bright
You are my star sweetheart
You fill my heart with love
You shine
The brightest of them all

YOU WERE THERE

For so long, there was no one there
Then you came along
You filled my days by simply being there
You made time that we may be together
Nothing else mattered
You cared
When I needed to talk
You were there
You gave me a listening ear
I thank you for the moments special and dear
For the laughter that we shared
Thank you
Words cannot explain my gratitude and appreciation to
you
Words simply cannot express just how much your
friendship means to me
I thank you for being there
But most of all
I thank you for simply being you

YOU

You promised me the sunshine
You wished away the storm
Took away the darkness and the rain
And with a flash brought light into my life again
You gave my life new meaning
Renewed my hope
Gave me a reason for believing
You were my narrow escape
You restored my faith
Gave me the strength and the courage to face each new
day
You were my mirror of belief
My silver lining
You are my reason for believing

FRIENDSHIP AND LOVE

For as sure as yesterday is gone and today is today
Friendship comes first in every way
And for love
Love is sharing
Not giving more than receiving
Not jealous or selfish
But freedom, understanding, trust and caring
Caring for one another
Showing each other affection
And love is deep and natural
But friendship takes time
Time to grow, time to mature and find its true meaning

For when it gets lonely as it sometimes do
Love comes calling
Calling for friendship, calling for you
And so many times those feelings are unanswered
They cuddle within and sadden the heart
When the little everyday things that matter
We so often neglect to say
I love you, thank you
Can simply help to make each other's day

So...
While I know you, I say thank you
I appreciate you, I love you and I care
I'll be good to you
For in you I have found a friend
A friend to treasure, a friend to share
And if friendship first is what you believe in, my dear
Then you my friend will see
That this dear old friendship begins with me

ALL OR NOT AT ALL

When I say I love you
I love you with the love
Of the Father in me
When I give
I give of and from the heart
As the Father gives to me
I know no other way
No other how
There's no halfway
I give my best, my all
All the way
Or not at all

HE

Man cannot control his heart
He can only protect it

How easy it is for man to hurt
When he is true to himself
True to his heart
How easy it is for him to cry
When he loves
How wonderful it is to say hello
When the heart is pounding with joy
And everything is just right
How hard it is
So hard, so sad to say goodbye
When the darkness closes in
And everything diminishes
The love he had is disappearing
Right before his very eyes
How easy it is for man to hurt

Man cannot control his heart
He can only try to protect it

HURT WITHOUT A CAUSE

I love you
But what can I do
The distance gets closer
But not near enough
The madness seems far
But near to hurt

I´m sorry
But what good does that do
Broken hearts only feel the pain
Each day more lost, less gained
I believe in to forgive and try to forget
But you believe in holding out
What can I say

Time cannot erase the past
Time will not wipe away these tears I cry at last
Today is too soon
Too soon to ease the pain that yesterday regrets
Tomorrow is too late
Much too late to stop the pain without intent to hurt

I love you...
I love you with all my heart

RISKING IT ALL

My loving you has recreated me
And my spirit soars through many miles of sky and over
distant seas to be with you

My loving you has given me the courage
To spread my wings and fly like an eagle
Taking me to new heights
And I am just learning again in a long time
To take a chance
Giving my life new meaning
Feeling like a child
Learning to love
Learning to smile
Learning to cry

My loving you makes me happy
Makes me sad
Makes me afraid and confused
Makes me mad...about me, about you
Never before have I felt this way
Letting myself go
Feeling the way I do about you, about me
But I am so much more than a child now
Falling in love
Emotions like blood rushing through my veins
And this feeling so warm soothing my heart is just a
crying shame
For with every heartbeat it speaks a warning of
unsuspected pain

Remembering how to cry...again
Wanting to believe...again
Giving into love

I want to reach out and touch you
Gently, affectionately, unexpectedly
I want to kiss you
Softly, sweetly, only shortly
My loving you makes me want to do things
All the little things young lovers do
Makes me want to love you
Passionately make love to you
My loving you makes me weak, sustains me
But you loving me would make my world complete
So, I´m risking it all
Remembering how it feels to hurt
Reminiscing the pain of a broken heart
Hoping, praying that you´ll love me back

SAY YES

It's easy to fall in love with the extraordinary
Life is full of surprises
Yours and mine
And every tomorrow a window of hope
When we say yes

There's passion but no compassion
Lust but no love
Still love could be the answer to all our problems
Yours and mine
When we say yes

When we say yes
Love is quick to respond
And love could also be unkind
It hurts
But love is patient, eternal and strong
When we say yes

Say yes

TRYING TO FORGET

It should have been me
To walk away from you
It should have been me
To set you free

Trying to forget the love
That just won´t let me forget
You´ve set me free without any reasons
So many questions
Unequal answers
And you don´t care to listen
So how can I forget

Trying to forget the love
Laughing the tears away
Hiding behind the fears
Making excuses
Substituting love
Being satisfied with less
Thinking I´ve won
Realizing I just can´t
Forget the love

It should have been me
It should have been me

FOR THE LOVE OF YOU

You´ve shared my soul, my heart
You brought out the best in me
The sweetest part
And seen the worst of me
Beautiful and special as you are
With love so unconditional and rare
Wherever I go, whatever I do
In all of me
There will always be a part of you

SILENT PAIN

Never before have I needed a love like I need your love
You make it so easy to give
Without confession or guilt, I give
Freely and without reservation, I give
No one can ask for more
But you hurt me and hurt me

These tears and laughter we shared were real, delightful
and sweet
Your childlike and easy ways I cannot forget
Your love that made my life complete
Will haunt me the rest of my days
For the thought of no more
Will hurt me and hurt me

Change has come, I feel
All else has failed it seems
And I fear a new vision
All I have is the past
To live in the past is to be with you
Only then can my heart really be true
But I reach out and feel, live only the memories of you
Moments that once touched my heart
Warmed my heart
Memories real and alive as any man that ever lived
One by one they come to me
They are my comfort, my grief, my all
They will stay with me all of my days and haunt me

This heart has loved as much as it has hurt and more
Weathering storms and standing in the eye of many
hurricanes
And I know, I pray that love will call your name again
I know that it's only my will I can depend on
For go on I must
But it's the good times I can't trust
All I ask is a smile from you
A pleasant word or two
Only now and then
That's all

MISSING YOU

I want to write every day
I want every time to say
I love you
Oh! How I miss you
I want to reach out and touch you
But nothing´s changed
Nothing´s new
Only the distance grows and grows
While I miss you

WITHOUT YOU

I thought that I couldn´t live without your love
I thought that dying was the only way out
I was out on the ledge
Fearing the dreadful fall of eternal loss
I thought that there was no other one for me
Without you I was afraid just what life would be
Didn´t want to be free
I was afraid that after you
There would be no more me
Before me was the misery
Couldn´t see that without you
There would still be a me
Didn´t know that I could be happy
I was blind
I was so wrong
I thank God
Come rain but too comes shine
Now I´m so glad that I could feel the pain
Lets me know that I am living again

LETTING GO

My biggest weakness
Not knowing how to let go
Couldn´t believe that love so strong was o´er
We said goodbye almost as we said hello
For so long I was sore
Didn´t understand
Didn´t recognize the times
There´s a time to love
And a time to let go
Now that we are apart
The end seems only the start
I loved you not only for your body
But for the gift of fulfilment you gave to me
My body and my soul
I love you now even more
For loving me enough
To let me go

STRONG

Strong
I have to be strong
You let me down
You took your love and moved along
And my love is ever so strong

Why
What have I done
You treat me so wrong
Your love is gone
I am weak
But I must be strong
Strong to go on

LOST CHILD

"I'm not sorry for myself," she said
"I am lonely and sad
Lonely and lost like a child without a home
In a world with so many people
I stand alone
Born to wander and roam"

She knows not from where she comes
She asks herself, "Where do I belong?"
She's young and fine
She's waiting
Hoping for someone to come
And take her hand
And lead her on
To a place...
A place...
A place...

WHO AM I

I am me
Created, made and brought into this world
By a man and a woman of substance, my parents
Yet I know not who I am

I am thirteen
Here is where I live
I call it home
But what is home
Comfort, happiness, love and friendship
Or quarrels, fights and madness
I do not know
Just not sure
For I only live here
It´s not my own

I live, life
Only half-full
So many things I do not comprehend
Things I see, emotions that come to me
Pain and hurt; joy and sorrow; love and hate
Mutual love, fatal love
And does the world really care
Marriages, divorces, so much killing
Filling the stage with its many faces and foolish
disguises

Now I am grown up
I am a woman, a wife and a mother
I am no longer my parents' child
But was I ever
They do not understand

Who am I
Who am I really
Why
I am God´s child
I am God´s pride

BE

I ask only for my heart
That it may seek the right to love freely
Without confession or guilt
Or fear of hurting
I only ask that my heart be set free and be
Whatever it can...be

I may do the same for me
That I may be...free
Free of the greyness that hovers me
Free of the blindness that I may one day see
No more gloomy darkness of uncertainties
Only blue skies, daydreams and fantasies
No more bittersweet memories of a love
That may never...be

FORSAKEN HEART

Love has gone but memories live on

For when we were just the knowledge of each other
We were nothing but-
Loving and friendly, laughing intimacies of one another
But after we have given a part of ourselves so desirable
to each other
The friendliness, the warmth, the charms and the smiles
have all disappeared
so ruthlessly onto the surface of your fearful and
troubled mind
And alien my love to your heart

Nothing hurts more than that of an estranged love
Misunderstood and advantageous
stolen and discreet
But the painful truth of longing, wanting
Remains firm without receiving
And my body trembles for you
My whole being weakens for the irresistible love of you
Tender eyes are forced to turn away from thee
When a little heart is weeping and wailing for a smile
from thee
And loving arms reaching, searching for that gentle
touch
A lasting touch that won´t ever go away from me

And though I know I can´t undo the past
Though I know that this love was not meant to last
My fragile heart, now breaking heart
Steals a silent, secret wish to start anew
Retract and make a fresh start
But that´s just that
And the memories I must live with
For fear of losing thee eternally

O´sweetest love
Return to me
And let the passing time be not my enemy
I'm calling, calling in the name of love
For fear that hate will take its place
And leave this forsaken heart
Without a trace
Without hope
Without a smile upon its face

You hide for fear that I may seek you, but it is in hiding
that I will seek to find you

AGAIN

The fault is all mine
Loving you
You loving me
But like a new born
Love is blind
And if / should I have the chance
To do it all over again
I wouldn´t hesitate
. I´d go right ahead
And make the same mistake...again

GOOD TIMES

So many goodbyes have passed between us
So many sad goodbyes
If this must be the last
Then let me cry again
Just this once
One last time
For the good times

So many yesterdays
So many wonderful yesterdays
If there must be no more tomorrows
Then let me turn the pages back a little
Take one last trip down memory lane
Let me smile again
Sigh a little
Every time I remember the good times

So many smiles
So many warm and tender smiles

BEST FRIENDS

You and I have done
Have shared some of the most wonderful moments in
time
Times that we may never dare with anyone else
Those beautiful and endless memories are priceless
treasures I´ve found with you
And no one can take them away
If we can´t be anything more but...
If we can´t be together
Let´s not lose each other
Let´s be friends
After all
Best friends are the second best

LIFE IS TOO SHORT

Life is too short to be angry
Life is too short to live in fear
And sometimes though life may seem hard
Life too is beautiful
So let's not waste time being enemies

I am willing to be your friend
If you will be mine
If you are strong enough to give us a chance
Then I am willing to go the distance
Right here, right now
But don't delay
Life is too short to wait

If all I can do is make you smile
Then it would be worth the while
If the sound of my voice brings you cheer
Then it's the least I can share
If my being there or a chance that you might be there
brings you joy
Then I'll be one happy girl and you, one happy boy
If spending time together makes your world a little
better, a little happier
There's no reason why this friendship should be made a
sunder
But don't give up
Life is too short for goodbyes

Life is too short to fret and frown
We can't all win the crown
But we can all wear the crown, of LIFE

THE FIRST TIME

The first time you told me that you love me
I believed you
Since then a lot has happened
A lot has been said
But that hasn´t changed the line

The first time you said that you´ll always love me
I was convinced
It took no effort
I took it with ease
Since then a lot more has occurred
Even more has been said
But that hasn´t changed a single word

There´s no better time, no surer time
Than the first time
When in doubt
I close my eyes
Memories of that first time crowd my mind
Every second of the moment
Every sweet, little word I hear
And the message is clear

My ears cannot forget the whisper
The sound of forever
The sweetest sound in my ear
Each time
Like the first time

DO YOU

Do you turn the memories in your head that we shared
Do you take them one by one
Share a smile or a tear
Do you feel the pain I feel for you
The same pain
And cry the same tears too
Do you miss me
Think of me
Do you see all your thoughts and wishes coming through
And when you dream
Do you dream of forever you and me

Do you wonder if I am wondering about you
Get lonely
Sigh for me
Or are you in the arms of someone new
Do you dream of you and I like turtle doves
on feathered clouds so high
Do you wake up in the middle of the night
and call my name out loud
And when you pray
Do you get down on your knees
And cry out in the name of love
Do you believe in fairy tales, white knights and fantasies
In miracles and in love forever true
Do you

LONELY DREAMER

Sometimes all I ask for is what we had
All I ask is that our hearts be glad
But that´s a lonely quest
Lonely and sad

Once you gave me a dream
A dream of hope
A dream for two
Something to hold on to
But you walked out of that dream
In all its glory
All its bloom
You walked out of our dream

Sometimes I feel
I could break down and cry
Sometimes I try so hard to hide the pain
The tears I cannot find

Once I had a dream
I shared this dream
But now I´m left here on my own
To dream alone

FOREVER TO YOU

A prayer of love

Each night I pray
I say a little prayer for you
I pray that although the distance keeps us apart
And though people grow sometimes apart
That our hearts may always find a way to touch
That the sparks that once burned to flames
May rekindle and burn again and again
I pray that we may kiss the bittersweet tears from each
other's cheek each time we meet
And that we'll find again the joy and laughter as we
greet
The love we once shared was precious
The magic was sweet
And in our hearts we held the keys that made life so
complete
As the night sleeps
I pray that every dream you dream, every heartbeat will
bring us closer together
And that in the hope of every positive thought
Along the same path
We'll find our way back to each other
With every breath I take, I pray
That the loss you feared
The hurt you shared
Will be burnt away in the furnace of new discoveries
And life will start afresh on greener prairies
It's just a little whisper
Each time I think of you

And every moment that you stay away, I pray
That you'll guard the key to your heart
Break the barriers of love and make a new start
I pray that your heart will remain open to love,
understanding, forgiveness
Open to me
For together as one we are stronger
And together we will conquer
A whole new world is opening up here
And so I pray
That our lives will be furnished with new hopes, new
dreams to pursue, new beginnings, new ventures and a
love that would last forever
That's my wish for you
And if, should forever be true
Then I give it to you
Baby, bring it home to me
Cause I can't think of a better couple
To give forever to

FANTASY FRIEND

I´m searching for the friendship ignited only in my mind
But this friendship needs a friend
And this friend doesn´t want to be found
Like a volcano
Bubbling, ready to explode
This girl wants more

Everybody needs somebody
It seems unfortunately for me
That my somebody is you

DAD

The tragedy is all mine
Dad
I´ll never call your name
I´ll never say the word
Dad
My friends do not know the pain
For them, pictionary is just another imaginary game
Dad
You understand
For me it´s just not the same
I was only a baby
Blind and lame
You left me without reason
Without a name
Dad
Who should I blame
Take away the constant longing
Dad
Give me just one chance to call you
Dad

YOU SLEEP

Going home
I know you´re home
But you sleep
In the darkness
I see your face
You smile
But I weep

Oh! How I wish
Just for one more day
Oh! How I´d like to touch you
So many things I´d like to say
But you sleep
Six feet deep
You sleep

In a world without you
I´m so alone
´Cause you sleep
You've left me here on my own
Without warning
Without a clue
You sleep
And this is all new to me
I do not understand
Why you sleep
And I´m blue
Blue while you sleep

FOUR WALLS

It is especially these afternoons
When it´s cold outside
When it´s raining outside
When it snows outside
These days when I stay at home
That I feel alone

It is especially these afternoons
When the sun´s shining
The air is warm
And the music I´m listening is just for two
That I think of you

It is especially these afternoons
When I can hear the drops of the rain
When I can see the falling snow
And the sun´s rays bursting out with glow
Then I turn the music down low
I turn the lights off
I close my eyes
And still I can see a light
Shining on you
Like a spot in my heart

It is especially these afternoons
When you are here with me
That everything´s so complete
It will be especially these afternoons
When you are no longer here with me
When my heart´s weary with thoughts of you
That I´ll be missing you

When four walls close me in
And sleep won´t come
You´ll hear me call your name
Across the seas you´ll hear it again and again
And in your heart you´ll know
That I´ll be missing you so

Nesta Rüegg / Thomas Strini

JUST HOW MUCH I LOVE YOU

When the feelings so strong
When I love yous been said a thousand times before
When the words seem right
But they just don´t say much more
He lets his body talk to me
"Let´s make love," says he
"Let me show you
Just how much I love you"

THE GIFT

Created out of love
Resulting in love, a gift
Of happiness, of experience to be gained, of endless and
overwhelming joy
So I am told
A gift given unto me
I know not what it is or where it comes from
A surprise, carefully disguised, wrapped up so securely
Simple, no colourful paper or tied up with pretty bows
But the awareness polishes my curiosity and leaves me
with a special glow
So I am told
Happy, glowing, eager, impatient
I can feel it, almost touch it in my imagination
But I must remain patient and calm
Visualizing it I can´t
I´m guessing that´s all I can
But I sense that it is precious and unique just for me
This gift I´m told will soon unfold
But I must carefully unwrap its-not-so-attractive package
Cut the attached string and all will be revealed to me
I´m told
But what have I done to deserve such a gift
Have I lived so well
Loved so well
And why me, why now
And what is this secret, this so well hidden gift
Alas
The time has come
It breathes a sigh of relief, of joy, of sweet and long
awaited suspicion, mixed emotions
And oh what a revelation. What a wondrous and blessed
gift

A gift of life, of family
A gift of chance, ever changing, ever challenging
A gift of completion
Completing my existence and making me more than
what I already am
Child of God, daughter
Sister, woman, wife...MOTHER
A gift of parenting
A gift of motherhood

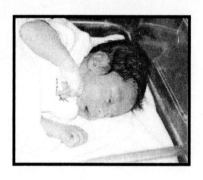

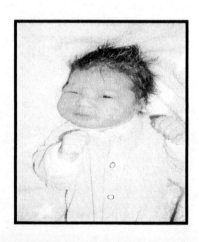

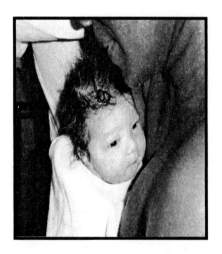

I've felt the pain, but with this pain came a deeper understanding, a deeper love, a love like no other. Pain that brought joy

TENDER APPRECIATION

For Stefan & Sabrina

Dear Father
You have created me in your own image and likeness
I am beautiful in your eyes if no other
In your eyes I am perfect even with flaws
You've moulded me, formed me
And bless me with unconditional love
You´ve showered me with gifts
The greatest of these being life
You´ve given me parents
Precious gems to treasure
And many share only half the pleasure
You watch over me all the time
Providing me with constant guidance and protection
Friendship and an everlasting companion
Thank you for giving me a chance
For securing a place for me in your plan
No matter what I do or where I go
You will always love me, I know
I can call on you all the time, anytime
I know you're there waiting for my call
Listening without interruption, always patient, always
kind
Oh Father of all fathers
Who sees all and knows all
My wants, my needs, my longings

My fears, my cries, my joys
My unforeseen wrongdoings
Ever loving, ever forgiving, ever understanding
Heavenly Father
I love me
I love you for loving me
I am just a baby
Happy and carefree
Continue to guide me from above
Help me to grow in love
Help me to embrace the world with an open heart
Help me to be like you
Amen

BORROWED LOVE

To hurt or not to hurt
That is the question
But to think of all those wonderful moments we shared
together
Must leave a trace of emptiness and loss
´Cause we took a chance
Took into our arms what didn´t belong to us and
welcomed it with joy
Now we must pay the price of borrowed love

Lack of wisdom led us to use our hearts and not our
heads
Made us selfish and inconsiderate
To share the good and intimate feelings
The can´t-take-it, lonesome feelings
That led us to an uncontrollable situation
Of pretence, lies and unanswered questions
And the pain and hardships await us
Of borrowed love

WHEN I THINK OF YOU

When I think of you
I think of the little and sweet things you do
For you I wear a smile in my heart

When I think of you
I´m overwhelmed with affection
To hold you close
Just to hold your hand
Warms my heart inside

When I think of you
I think of friendship
I think of love
A single thought can mean so much
When you are away

When I think of you
I´m lost on the pleasant highway down memory lane
Going no where
And nothing seems the same
But the sweet whisper of my name
The thought that you´ll be coming home
Fills my heart with joy
Every thought of you
Makes me want to jump for you
When I think of you

I WANT TO LAUGH

I want to laugh
I want to sing
I want to wake up in the morning
With lots of zeal
And do lots of things

I want to be happy
I want to reach deep within
Touch my happiness
And know that it´s real
I want to laugh

WHO KNOWS

Who knows what tomorrow will bring
Who knows when heaven's bells will ring
I only know there are oceans, there are streams
There are rivers and there are seas
But no mama, no mama's dreams

Who will hear my cry
Who will dry my eyes
Who'll make everything alright

Who knows what the wind blows
Who knows where the lonely souls go
Perhaps beyond there's a greater love
That only the lonely knows
While we are left here to mourn and wonder
Who knows…

Are you happy
Are you sad
Are you warm
Is someone holding you, mama

Memories you are here
You surround me
Every image, every sound you make is in my ear
I hear your call
But it's dark and I cannot see
I cannot seem to find the place you hide from me

Who can hear your cry
Who will dry your eyes
Who will share your sweet smile

Mama
Please come back to me
Come to the light
And let me see

CRY

Cry if you must
No need to even try
Let the tears run free from your eyes
And cry

Cry a well of tears if you care
Don´t hold back
The moment is here
Let it go
Let it flow
Just cry

Cry with confidence
Cry with pride
Reach for the clouds
Cry

Cry out loud
Let the power take you there
You have nothing to fear
Know that your freedom lies in your tears
And cry

RIVER OF JOY

I go down to the waters
In the still of the night
I hope to find myself
But it´s only am empty river I find
Amidst the shadows in the darkness
I hide myself
And beauty in all it´s splendour and completeness
Only half shared
I cry me a river
A river of joy

GOODBYE

Strange
That I knew loneliness long before I met you
Strange
That I knew pain long before you came
But it never gets easier
It´s either worse
Or the same

Strange
How goodbye, an old friend of mine
The only one of its kind
He comes and comes
But it´s never my favourite time

Strange
The tears I cry are yours and mine
But you don´t see them
You walk away and leave them behind
Strange
That you think I´ll be just fine

THE FLIGHT

I love you
I love you dearly
I will love you 'til I die

Soon it is dawn
A new day
And I must board a plane
Take a flight and fly away
But not to you
You are so much farther away

I can think of a thousand things
I´d like to say
But you wouldn´t listen
If He that giveth life
Thou taketh away, I pray
That my love reaches you
Touches you
In every way

IF I SHOULD DIE

If I should die
Think only this of me
That there is some love of a foreign field
That is forever yours

There shall be in that rich earth
The truest love concealed
A love I bore
Grew to know and made aware
Gave once that heart to love
Its ways to roam
A body of full and complete passion
Sweet sensations and desires
That would burn the foreign love of old

And think
This heart, all love burns away
Nourishes the rich earth
Making it richer than before
And the wonder of my love
The clouds cry
The sun shines
The flowers grow
And the earth flourishes
Into a paradise

DON´T MOURN FOR ME

When I am dead and gone
To whom shall my love belong
The memories will live on
Like music without a song
Don´t mourn for me

And to those I may leave behind
Have no pity
In all of you will remain a part of me
A new chapter of life has begun
With little choice to none
We are all aware that this time must come

The journey is long
But with every beginning there´s an end
And with every step of the way
We are stronger

The pain evolves
The loss is like the remains after a storm
But everything comes to pass
Don´t grieve for me
Don´t mourn for me

Life goes on
Full of so much beautiful colours
And beautiful things

THE BATTLE

So many battles fought
We´ve won a few and some we´ve lost
But the battle continues
Emotions rocketing to the sky
Cupid´s arrow shooting from both sides
Every heartbeat´s a cannon ball bombarding the walls of
my heart
And I´m standing here
Looking on from the inside of the gates of hell
Unexpected attack resulting in bitter-sweet conquer
We lay down our arms but we do not surrender
We close the gates but we do not shut them
And we´re standing by
Looking on from the outside of the gates of hell
Here we are
The inseparable, separated
The untouchables, defeated
Oh feelings, soldiers of my heart
Be on guard
Dynamite of memories running through my veins
One little spark and the explosions of my heart´s bigger
than my brains
Oh love, flame of my being burning up in a heart of hell
Cease fire
This heart has been burnt too many times before
Don´t want to be burnt no more
Oh pain, enemy of my heart
Draw back
No more attack

Though I know to lose this battle
I must pay the penalty
Captured by my very own soldiers
To suffer, punished and tortured for the sins of my heart
I must lay down my life on the line
For love is my only weapon
And I am not strong enough to give up
A deadly price to pay
Oh commitment, sin of my heart
Always loving you, right from the very start
Is this the only way
Oh enemy, fiend of my soul
End this struggle, leave me alone
This rival has changed its course, found a new source
I can´t fight anymore
There are no winners, no losers in this war of hell
Only prisoners of love
Surrendering to second best

BROKEN PIECES

I gave you my love
The weapon to my heart
Thought that my loving you would make me happy
That my love was strong enough to hold you
I wasn´t smart
I gave you my little heaven on earth
Without questions
Without reasons
I gave you my heart
But you ached it
And as if that wasn´t enough
You broke it
And gave it back in pieces

Love is the one thing you can give and yet keep and I
thank God for that, for I would lose it all

WRECKED

There is a storm in my heart
A river flowing from my eyes
A pool everywhere I stand
And you on my mind

I´M JEALOUS OF THE NIGHT   1

I´m jealous of the night caressing you
Like the tender lips of a baby
Caress his mother´s breast
I´m jealous of the night
Holding you close
With its every power and force
Taking you fully into its control

I´m jealous, jealous of the night
Of every moment spent with you
Of the private affair
So intimate, so true
In the long darkness
It turns you up
Like the ploughman ploughs the soil
And discovers your most secret dreams
Your soul

I´m jealous, jealous like hell
Guilty and condemned
Cast down by its darkest spell
´Cause I´m jealous
´Cause I´m jealous
I´m like a prisoner in a cell
And the jealousy locked away inside
I remain guilty as charged
And only time will tell
Only time can break this awful spell
That makes me jealous
Jealous of the night

ONLY FOR YOU

This fire that burns in my soul
Burns only for you
These tears I cry that emerge from the depth of me
Flow only for you
These eyes that turn the whole world upside down
Are searching only for you
These arms, open, empty arms stretching far and wide
Wanting just to hold you
Are reaching for no one new
Only for you

HEART

Let me suffer not the pains of love
Let me live for the joys of loving
Let me rejoice in the morning
Give praise in the evening
For this warm and wonderful feeling
Let me forget not the passion
The sweetness, dear heart
You let me know love
As no other heart has ever known
You let me take another heart
And make it my own
Heart
Let me not alone

THANK YOU

Let the words in my heart speak with ease
Let my heart say exactly how it feels
Thank you
For being there
Your company warm and thrilling
And you always willing, always pleasing
Thank you
You´ve filled my days like you´d never know
But now you have to go
Thank you
For sharing in my wildest thoughts
My dreams, my music, my laughter
Thank you
For giving me the right
To know you better

DOWN MEMORY LANE / I REMEMBER...

I remember sometimes at assembly when you would
break down and leave the hall
I remember how unsympathetic some of the girls were
and said that you're not so strong after all
I remember how I felt and thought that she's just human
And the result of your action created a happy wish in me
Determined to be your friend
To smile at you
Talk with you
But at the same time
To heed to your demands /commands

I remember what joy I felt to run to town and find the
right card, the perfect item that would please you
I remember how I "pick and choose" so carefully, so
personally
I remember how we talked and when we talked
I remember how you listened
How with every breath you tried
And sometimes how I cried
I remember how well you grew to know and understand
me and how well too you accepted my honesty and
freedom of speech
Even though at times perhaps it wasn't quite what you
would have liked to hear
But you never ceased to care

I remember that hot summer day in your office
The day I predicted that sadness in your eyes
I remember how you laughed so free and with such ease
And I too was almost fooled by such disguise, such
laughter
I remember thinking that I can make her laugh just
simply being me
WAW!   How wonderful
And at last you opened up to me
And I remember how at times you opened up my whole
world too

I remember all those times
All those yesterdays down memory lane
And long for more tomorrows

Tribute to Sr. Gabrielle Mason
Ex-Principal
St. Joseph's convent (St. George's)
25th Jubilee

YOU GAVE ME THAT

You gave me what I was missing
A taste of adventure
A chance worth taking
And moments that add meaning to the life I was living

You showered me with affection
Each gentle touch
Each unspoken word
Each sweet, little thought has meant so much
The endless attention
The imaginary flowers
The song that warmed my heart
You gave me that

You brought me laughter
You coloured my smile
And though it took me time to give my heart
You remained patient and satisfied
Kept me close, held me gently but tight
You never gave up ....

I brought you laughter
I discovered your smile
I made you happy just being at your side
But you, you gave me love
Right from the start
You gave me that

THE PROMISE

I love when you say, I love you
I love that you love me, that you care
And the way you give to me pure, simple and true
How can I tell you

I love your smile and every moment spent with you
makes it all worthwhile
I love the way you give to me, no reservation, no
mystery
How can I give back to you

Chances come and chances go
Some we keep and some we let go
But as crazy as it seems the chance was all on me
You won my heart with ease

I love when I say, I love you
I love the sound, the response I hear
I love all that we share
Together we laugh, cry and hurt
But together we love
And I am so lucky that you choose to give to me
To love me and share with me so completely
Oh how I love the way you give to me
How can I ever give back to you

The moment is here, the test of time
This moment we give to chance, to love
When our arms would feel its lonely embrace
And our lips long to share the company of a kiss
So beautiful, so sweet
When we say not goodbye but `til we meet again
I love the way we love together
But a half is not a whole without the other
How I'll miss you
I'll love the way you'll miss me too
But I'll pray that the day will soon come when you'll
return
And I've learned
I promise to give it all back to you

´Cause I love the way I love you
I love the way it makes me feel
And I want to give it all to you

BECAUSE

Because you are the melody in my song
The treasure in my heart
Because you are my sunrise, my sunset
My little heaven on earth
Because you are all that and so much more
Is still no reason why I love you so

Because you are my only rose in the winter snow
Because your love fills my soul
Everywhere I go, I´m never alone
Because you are my positive motivation
My today, my tomorrow
Somehow we belong

Because we are together
Because you share the pain that we suffer
Because you are my now
I´m as happy as can be
Because, because, because
Just because you´re mine

IF

If there were no yesterday
All would be well today
But there was a yesterday
And from now on
Today and tomorrow will never be the same

Yesterday was a mistake with all its fun and games
Tomorrow will be new games to play
Oh day of days
How many todays and tomorrows will be just that
yesterday

If you were the only boy and I, the only girl
If tears were laughter and prayers were answers
And yesterday was ours
Then ours would be the perfect love
If only yesterday never was

COLD HEART

Time and time again you´ve told me
But I wouldn´t listen
You´ve said it once, twice
All the things you´ve said before
I´ll hear them once more
In your cold, bitter cold words of ice

You´ve written me letters
I´ve read them out loud
Those cold, beastly, cold words of ice
How they froze my heart
Leaving me numb inside
Every word right from the start

You´ve drawn me pictures
Black and white
Opened my eyes that I may see the light
But this heart´s shut tight
Cold, blinded by your freezing words of ice

Day after day
Time after time
I seek the warmth in your eyes
In your voice
But with time I´ve realized
The only thing on your mind
Are your cold, winter, cold words of ice

DEATH

Your love I have no more
What a sad way to go
I see only the night
The darkness
No light at the end
I see death
I think death
For death is within me
Cold and silent is the way of my heart
The travel is slow and the love far behind
Fading away as I go
The darkness is nearer and the heart weaker
Never as before
No more cries can be heard
No more pain can be felt
Death is now a welcomed comfort
This heart is no more
Free of the world
Free of the love that brought me to death
Free of hurt
FREE

FOREVER IS WITHOUT END

The time has come without a chance for goodbye
Nothing's plan for us and while we live
Love is for the giving
There will be no goodbyes, no mournful sighs
And time to cry
Forever is without end
And so is my love for you

But...
Where will you be
Where will you be
When I can no longer feel your tight squeeze
Your soft lips only a dream
When I can no longer hear the sound of your laughter
Your heartbeat knocking against my heart like thunder
Where will you be

Where will you be
When I can no longer see your smile
The love light in your eyes
Only a memory, only a lie
Where will you be
Will you still love me

Forever is without end
And so is my love for you

MY HEART KNOWS

For as long as my heart can remember
It has loved you
And for every time I loved you
I hurt a thousand times
For every time I smiled with you
I cried a thousand tears
My heart knows

Heaven knows I love you
Heaven knows I care
Heaven knows I pay with every heartbeat I share
Burning up with desires
Holding back the fears
Reaching out with feelings
Only my heart knows

It takes a big and strong heart to love you
Keep on loving you, but I do
My heart knows
And so few hearts know love so genuine and true
Yet this poor heart lies deep and blue
And you and I both know
Just how deep and long true love can go
Can't you see
This heart beats only for you
And will the memories ever end
Will this heart ever love the same again
Only my heart knows

ANGRY HEART

I would have been ready to leave my old world
And start a whole new life with you
But loving you hurts so much
I sometimes wonder if I´m just not loving you enough
But what is enough
How can one measure enough

I would have given my life away that I might have your
love today
But this thought is no more
The love never dies
The dream stays alive
Hell, this fight is o´er

How many more chances do you need
Seventy times seventy I forgive
How many more times must I give in
No, no more apologies
Love is just too easy to forgive
For the longest while my heart belonged to you
Remained true to you
Waiting for the moment when you´d take me into your
arms
Make me your one and only
And the whole world would stop turning
For the longest while I was just a fool in love with you
Each time I kept losing my mind
Holding on
Waiting for a chance, waiting for change
But change never comes

And the hurt never gets easier for me
I´m always the one to try
Always the one to cry
But that was yesterday, dead and gone
This fool´s moving along
For this angry heart, though still hungers for you
No longer aches for you

Love without hope is but bitter luck
I don´t give a ......
Now I know
I´ve learnt that love on it´s own is a long and weary trip
But this heart's tired of falling in the same old pit
And I´ve learned that time doesn´t heal
It opens eyes
It shines light on the reality
And whoever said that love is blind
Better think twice
´Cause love is just another excuse for being stupid
Just another stupid reason for giving

ONLY DREAMING

For so long I watched and waited for you
But I only waited
Hour after hour I listened
I wished sweet things
But they were only wishes
As time rolled by I put everything aside
But they only stayed aside
All day long I dream
I see things
When I listened, I heard things
But when I looked
My heart´s ticking
And as I wished
Still there was nothing

How much guilt can one bear
How can one question another man´s freedom
Yes my hands are tied
But my heart´s open with love for you
Sure making excuses eases the pain
And a simple thought
A pleasant word
Consoles the heart lonely without love
Still never giving up
Day after day
Watching and waiting for you
As though you were my very own
For so long
Watching and waiting only in vain

FOOLS IN LOVE

Why do I cry
All the tears in the world
Didn't save this love of ours

Why do I hurt
Hurting is just too much
All my love couldn't make you stay
All the pain won't bring back yesterday

Why do I wait
Time is only a sinless game
All loss, no gain
And I'm waiting in hopeful vain

Why should I pay
For the price of your love
All the money in the world
Couldn't buy your love
All the love in my heart
Didn't win your love

Why do I hope
Heaven knows I just can't cope

I thought I understood
I thought we had it good
But you were just a fool
Who couldn't see
Just how true my love could be
And I was just a fool in love with you

Why do I feel ashamed
Why do I take the blame
For a love that's gone down the drain
Why should I be sorry
For a fool who's lost at his own game

I´M JEALOUS OF THE NIGHT   111

I´m jealous of the night
Because I´m only the day
With such a little role of love to play
I´m jealous
Of every sleepy night
Every little child
Every sweet lullaby
I´m jealous of the moonlight
And the way it looks into your eyes
Every twinkle of delight
Makes me jealous
Jealous of the night

I´m jealous of the night
Whispering sweet nothings in your ear
I´m jealous of every shooting star
And every secret wish that you share
I´m jealous of the night
With all its charm and grace
Overshadowing me
And I must hide my face
While it steps in and takes my place
I´m jealous
Jealous of the night

SLIP AWAY

Ours was a perfect love
A love few people ever dream of
And we the perfect pair
But you didn´t care
Took my love for granted and gambled our chance away
Now all I have left are the tears and memories of
yesterday

You gambled with your chances
You let them slip away
But the next chance I had
I gave my heart away

Still yesterday remains
My love´s ever the same
And my heart´s learning for the first time the real
meaning of pain

I could have taken the easy way out
Broken a few vows
Created my own miracle
Have everything I´ve ever dreamed about
But promises to love and obey
Gave my heart but one choice to stay

You gambled with our chances
You let them slip away
But the next chance I got
I gave my heart away

I chose character above love
Sacrificed my soul
And what I wanted to last forever
Only lasted a little while

Perhaps our time will come again
And this time may well be the last time
But until then
I´ll be living with "I do"
And living without you
´Cause I let you slip away too

CAN´T HIDE

I chose a life
That led me away from you
I gave up waiting on love
I gave up waiting on you
Because the words failed
And actions ceased to speak
I chose a life without you
Now no matter where I run to
I just can´t lose those memories
Why oh why
Why oh why me

OUR LOVE

When I am with you
I'm in a world of my own
A world of eternal flame
No water can out the fire that burns in my heart
Trapped is the eternal flame of our love
Burning in our hearts, body and soul
The explosions of feelings
No earthly heart can control
When I'm with you
In a world of our own
A world of unquenchable thirst
No water sweet enough can quench such thirst
But love…
Our love

THE AFFAIR

I gave then without thinking
Body, heart and soul
I loved you as my very own
I didn´t try to find control
Didn´t stop to think it o´er
Now that I am older and wiser
I see things differently, clearer
I know now what it meant
I know now what I did
I am not sorry
A crime of passion
A crime I committed
But I won´t dwell in a house of guilt
No
Looking back
I have no regrets
The love we shared belonged to us

And though love is shared doesn´t mean that love is less

WHERE DOES THIS LOVE LEAD

Where does this love lead
Where today´s passion is tomorrow´s confession
Where old memories cradled in our hearts
Turn into sweet thoughts of temptation
Where sad goodbyes and tear-filled eyes
Won´t wash away the pains of our emotions

Where...
Where does this love lead
To a far away distant land
Where only hearts can touch
Arms outstretched too far to clutch
Where sleepless nights and mournful days
Of wishful thinking and hopeless dreams delay the
whole life through
This love leads right back to you

DISTANCE

Though we are far away
Divided by many seas and miles of sky
In my heart I wear your smiles
Through its cruel space
I can see your face
In my thoughts you are there
The distance is still not far enough

Though it was just yesterday
It seems so far away
And I long for more memorable todays
Through its tunnel of silence
I can hear your voice, your whisper
In my mind you are there
The distance is still near enough

Time spent leaves much to be remembered
Quiet strolls not measured
As we walk through the promenade of life
In my mind it´s clear
Every footstep, your laughter resounding through the air
In its empty depth
I can feel your presence
I know you´re there
No distance so far or so high
So deep or so wide can come between us
No, no distance is far enough

I BLAME ME

Everyone deserves a second chance, I know
But I spoiled you with too many second chances, for
sure
Blame it on love
Don´t blame it on me

Just when I thought our dream had begun
It swiftly came to an end
And I blamed you
I blamed you for the missing parts of my happiness
My life, my completion
Because to my problems you were the only solution
I was convinced
Blame it on circumstance
Blame it on chance
Blame it on my Mother
Blame it on my heart for loving you
But don´t blame it on me

When you left me
I blamed you
For the vows I took
I blamed you

But as time allows me, I see
That even if it was meant to be
That I´m the one who set you free
So for righteousness sake
Blame it on me

I blame me for leaving you
I blame me for losing you
I blame me for not giving you
One last second chance

LET ME

Let me love
And if in loving I should lose myself
If in return no love should come
Then let me be thankful for the feeling
And let me try again

Let me give
And if in giving I should not receive
Let me be satisfied with just giving
But if in crying I should find myself again
Then let me rejoice in my tears

Let me smile
Let me laugh with you
And if this laughter brings you joy
Warms your heart inside
Then let me smile

DO YOU REMEMBER

I remember crouching into you lap
Cuddling into your arms
As I stargaze into the night
In a small place, your car
One summer night in November
Do you remember

I remember your touch
Your nail-bitten fingertips on my chin
The automatic closure of my lids
A slow moving gaze
A shared smile
A quick kiss as you drove
That summer night in November
Do you remember

I remember when we danced
How we danced
Your arms firm against my body
Holding me gently but tight
As our bodies became one
Our feet busy to the rhythm
And our hearts singing
Last summer night in November
Do you remember

TOGETHER

Together
You've known love
Together
You've vowed your love
Together
You'll know pain in its depths
And share in the joys of loving
Together
You'll rise to its highest ecstasy

Together
You'll roll in its bed of passion
And taste the sweetness at its core
Together
You'll greet the morn
And embrace the eye of twilight
Together
Day in and day out
True love
Basking in its rays of glory forevermore

Together, but apart
Each his own happiness
To discover and secure
But together as one
A love to nurture and grow

DOUBLE LIFE

No matter where life takes me
No matter what I do
I just don´t seem to shake you
Choosing to live the double life is my crime
Double the risk, double the fun
Double the time I´ll serve in return for loving you both
But living in the same world, separate lives
Not too far, just not too close
The acceptance is much for me to cope
So I made a different choice
To live the double life
Loving freely in secret
Secure and discreet
Perhaps love can justify all
But who is to judge
Each to his own selfishness and gain
Life is a gamble
Love is a game
We play to win but we lose all the same
Still I gave everything I had
Gave the best I knew how
I played, oh what a show I put on
But I lost anyhow
Whatever happened to yesterday
All we have is today
Where will we be tomorrow
Life is so short
You stop and give it too much thought you´re lost
But love is enormous
You give and give but it *lasts* and *lasts*

After all what more could I have said
What more could I do to keep from losing you
Still I lost you
Choices were made
But they were my choices
And I take full responsibility for choices that make me
happy
Partially or complete
Don´t know if I´ll ever be back on track
The better it is the harder it is to go back
And I want to believe
That the most loving thing my heart can do is set you
free, let you go
But it´s the unknown that holds me back, scares me so
But it is too, the hardest thing I´ll ever know

YOU WIN AGAIN

You played with my feelings
You dangled me like puppets on a string
You said goodbye
You thought you'd win
How dare you
Coming back here
Standing there
Playing with my weaknesses
You have the nerve
Trying to pursue a love
That you said was o'er
You say that our love is true
I say that I'm still in love with you
That I will always love you
That's the truth
In my eyes are the written proof
In my heart it's just no use
Damn you've played your game
You win again

I DECLARE

If I love thee with all my heart
Who on earth could tear it apart
If thee chooses to love me not
I will choose to love thee still
With all my heart and soul and mind
I will love thee

THE POWER OF LOVE

I have not arms so strong or fist so fine that I can fight. I am therefore not a fighter. I never was and I never will be.
Time and time again I have been hurt playing the game of life by words that fly like an arrow through the sky
But I survive

And when the heart is pierced, love must find a way either to conquer the pain, to hide the face of pain, face the face of pain or seek satisfaction in pain
I have tried all and have found my revenge in words
The very words that cut so deep like a knife
They are my arms and wrist
They are strong and they help me survive

In my own way I have enjoyed my fight. It gives satisfaction and consoles the heart for a moment, only a moment before the heart cries with regret
But still I survive

With maturity comes change and age brings reason, and neither is a threat but a challenge. When change comes about, one must accept and learn to live with it's newness. We cannot change each other. Sure we try but change must first come from within, within each individual only at the right and proper time

It is known that honesty is the best policy but sometimes I do wonder. The game of life is tough and so is simply being honest. I have lost a lot by simply being honest, but I have learned that I can't win it all

I have fought the pains and strains of this life with tears and prayers and sometimes too with anger and hatred in my heart; but the truth will set you free it is said. Yes, I believed and indeed I was free and a better person at least for me

Truth tells the whole story. Each added line, each painful broken rule and it hurts. There's no pretending, no denying it, but I will not lie. I will not hide behind a lie. I will not live a lie

Sometimes we have to be bigger than ourselves to overcome our trials, acknowledge our failures, admit our mistakes. To be able to stand up proudly and boldly and say "yes I did." Then we've won one more battle, conquered one more challenge and moved one step in the right direction. For as difficult as it may be, if we can do that without burying our heads in the sand, then it is one of the greatest achievements of the self and becoming who we are

Choices are ours to make. But sometimes we are forced to accept choices made. Things are not always the way we hope they'd be. Life doesn't come with a road map. Who knows where the road ends or what comes at the next bend. No one knows. One only knows the pain he feels and must endure. That's real. But there is always a window of hope. Another open door

How can one make one understand? How can one make one see looking through the pain that love is still a wonderful feeling to behold? And though feelings are shared, doesn't mean that love is less. For love is endless. I have learned to live in hope and positive thinking, for without it I would have nothing left.

What if we could turn back the "Hands of Time?" Turn a different corner? What if?

We ask ourselves, what is a world without love? What would this world be without pain? Is there a heart that doesn't know love? What is love?

Questions, questions and we keep on asking ourselves.

Sometimes when we look into each other's eyes, we see pain looking back at us and we tremble with fear, with regret, for this pain is so real, this pain we too can feel Everyone deserves a heart that knows happiness, a heart that's filled with love, one hundred percent true love

This is my story:

When he first came to me, I was drowning in tears, tears of many tomorrows, of pain; pain of loss, of remembrance of a love without a choice but to let go He reached out with his love, touched my heart and rescued me from the darkness He smiled and brought sunshine back into my life and his love kept me warm and safe From that moment I prayed to God that he may never go away and my prayers were answered too

I was scared but I was saved. Feeling safe and secure that with time my sick heart would begin to heal Like a kid and a new toy, never out of sight, never out of mind and then a bond is made Like the only star in the sky, shining, glowing, filled with happiness I'd never known, happiness I only dreamed of and blinded totally by love and present laughter that warmed my heart, I forgot for a moment that, which had thus caused me pain And so, I clung to that new toy. Still pleased, still overwhelmed with it's newness and love for it, I made a solemn vow "`til death do us part"

Then one day something happened. No, I didn't die but part of me was. Once more I was drowning. Falling deeper and deeper in that "hell-hole of depression", trying to hold on to the hope of a dream that would still one day come through and no one can help me now.

I'd fallen. Swallowed up in the darkness, lost but the way of my heart not forgotten. I made a choice. I turned a different corner. I cannot turn back the "Hands of Time"
So, what if…

Toys will be toys old or new but no two toys are the same. We cannot replace a loved toy. We cannot replace a love
But our hearts are not toys. We cannot just play dead, shut it off and wish all the feelings away
My heart will always be that same old heart of mine
Perhaps my whole life I will keep and cherish that new toy and in that same old heart the old toy, just loving it

So too, when love comes to us, we pray that it may never go away
In the drowning of our sorrow, love is the hand that reaches in
Lifts us out of the darkness into the light
Under the wings of love we can fly
In the warmth and tenderness of its care
It mends the broken pieces and soothes the pain
It turns our sorrow into joy
And our heart's a new found toy
Behind every dark cloud is a silver lining
Red roses blooming and colourful things

The game of life is survival
We must survive however we can
The human mind is strong
And so too is the heart, ever changing, ever growing

Yes, love can mend a broken heart. Love can change everything right from the start. Love can break a heart in a thousand parts

A THANKYOU PRAYER

From the dawn of morn to the peak of night
I lift up my hands to the Lord
I say Thank you
Thank you for dear life
For the air that I breathe
For everyday that I live
Thank you
For mother nature
For the birds of the air and the creatures of the earth
The flowers, the seasons and the trees
The rivers and the seas
Thank you for the rain
The sun that warms and shines so bright
The stars and moon that shine at night
Thank you
For mothers and fathers
Sisters and brothers
Nurses and doctors
Teachers and friends
I lift up my hands to the Lord
And I say
Thank you
For all my yesterdays and today
My sorrows and my pains
My losses and my gains
My grief and my fears
My hurts and my tears

For all my life catastrophes
My struggles and my challenges
My weaknesses and my strengths
My joy
I lift up my hands to the Lord
I say
Thank you
For they make me what I am today
Thank you for the hope of every new tomorrow

THE POET IN ME

The pain inflicted on me
The disappointments
The love that set me free
Have all inspired me
And brought out the poet in me

From life's experiences I've learnt
I've grown and I see
That regrets were born so that poems and sad songs can
be written
That which was, and what is, and what will be, will be
That which burdens my heart and crowd my head with
unthinkable thoughts
That, which brings out the poet in me

Had I never stood in the sun
And felt it's warmth upon my face
Had I never felt a loving embrace
Had I never stood in the rain
And bathe in its showers again and again
Had I never felt that thing called pain
And came face to face with its accomplice every now
and again
As it gently strikes my cheeks and shares a salty kiss
Had I not been blessed with this God-given gift
Then I couldn't write a line
About that or about this
Had I been understood
Had I had it good
Had I found my escape in all my sacrifices and
compromises I make
Had I…

In my youth
Along life's pathway
I took a walk with my heart
And discovered
The poet in me

IN THE END

Sometimes I may be wrong
Should you be strong, understand
Should you be there to take my hand
And lead me on
Should you scream and shout
In your effort to make things right again
Don't forget to say, 'I'm sorry"
In the end

Sometimes I may be blinded
May not see the things you want me to see
Be the way you want me to be
Should you be there
Should you lend me your eyes
Be rough about it and not realize
Don't forget to say you love me
In the end

Sometimes I may linger
May lose myself
Should you be there
Should you try to find me
And in your search be lost yourself
Should you find your way again
Don't forget to take me in your arms
In the end

ACKNOWLEDGEMENTS

I thank God for the gift of life, for the person I am today with all my faults and pride. I thank Him for his inspiration and the gift of expression with which He has blessed me; for the chance given me to love in its full capacity, discovering its highs and lows.
Thank you dear Lord for giving me the strength and courage to endure and journey through all the hurricanes of life, calm or turbulent and coming out stronger than ever.
Thank you for good friends, for good friends help weather the storms of life.

I thank you Mom for your love, your guidance and protection. You did your best to shelter me from the unexpected storms of life and nurtured me into adulthood. I know that you are somewhere up there watching over me and I hope that you are proud of me as I am of you.

My dear friends, you know who you are. I thank you for your love, understanding and acceptance.
For allowing me to share in your life as you share in mine and for playing such a significant role in my life. For your time and support; always a listening ear and a strong shoulder for my many tears. Thank you for sharing my experiences and yours ...good or bad. You know and understand my pain. For all the times I felt lost. When I needed something more than my loneliness and my tears. Thank you for encouraging me and believing in me. Thank you for always being there.

Cover Design by Markus Rueegg
My loving husband, What can I say??? Honey, I thank you for your artisitc input and incredible support in this my first book venture. For your unwavering love and understanding and for your extra big heart.

When all hope was lost and I was dying with my dreams, like God-sent you came along, took me under your blanket of love and gave me new hope, new dreams. You taught me that love is possible without pain. Through all my emotional turmoil's or "dramas" as you would say, that must have no doubt torn your own heart apart, you stood by me as no other man ever would. You keep on loving me. You help and support me and allow me at times the freedom of my heart.

Honey, you are true love and I love you.

Barbs´ thank you for coming through for me when I needed you the most and for making this dream come alive. For your support and sisterly love. You are very special to me and I love you more than you know.

Special thanks to Chris DeRiggs, Meryl Roberts-Marryshow, and to my publisher.